THOMAS & FRIENDS™

Hiro

Based on
The Railway Series
by the
Rev. W. Awdry

Illustrations by
Robin Davies

EGMONT

EGMONT

We bring stories to life

First published in Great Britain in 2016
by Egmont UK Limited
The Yellow Building, 1 Nicholas Road, London W11 4AN

Thomas the Tank Engine & Friends™

CREATED BY BRITT ALLCROFT

HiT entertainment

ISBN 978 1 4052 7985 7
62423/1
Printed in Italy

Stay safe online. Egmont is not responsible for content hosted by third parties.

Written by Emily Stead. Designed by Claire Yeo.
Series designed by Martin Aggett.

*This story is about Hiro,
an old engine who was lost for
many years. We wanted to help
fix Hiro, so he wouldn't be sent
for scrap, but we had to
keep him a secret . . .*

Spencer was visiting Sodor for the summer. He was helping to build a holiday home for the Duke and Duchess of Boxford.

"Out of my way, **slowcoach**!" he would shout. "I'm the **fastest, strongest** engine around!"

One day Spencer and Thomas had a contest to see who was strongest. "Whoever pulls his heavy load the furthest wins," said Spencer.

Thomas and Spencer were ready to race. **"Peep! Peep!"** whistled Edward, and they were off!

Spencer steamed ahead – but Thomas soon ran into trouble.

"My brakes have broken, I'm going too fast!" Thomas gasped.

He whooshed down a steep hill onto a rickety old track. Crashing through bushes, Thomas finally came to a stop.

When he opened his eyes, Thomas was surprised. There stood an engine, looking rusty and broken.

"My name is Hiro," said the old engine.

He told Thomas that he had come from far away. "I was the strongest engine there," said Hiro. "They called me the 'Master of the Railway'."

Thomas promised to fix Hiro and make him as good as new.

Thomas was so excited that he forgot all about Spencer!

He puffed slowly to the Steamworks so Victor could mend his brakes. When he got there, Thomas spotted a wagon with an old boiler.

"That's just **scrap**," Victor told Thomas.

"If we mended it, Hiro could have it!" thought Thomas.

Later, Thomas told Percy all about his new friend. Percy promised to keep Hiro a secret.

"If The Fat Controller finds out, he might send Hiro for **scrap**," Thomas worried.

So Thomas and Percy made a plan. Percy would do Thomas' jobs, while Thomas tried to fix Hiro.

Nosy Spencer wondered what they were up to!

When Thomas got home, he was in trouble. Percy had burst a safety valve pulling Thomas' train. The Fat Controller was cross.

"Why was Percy pulling your carriages?" he asked in a stern voice. "Now the mail is late."

Thomas felt **terrible**. He promised to help Percy with the mail train the next morning.

Thomas knew he needed his friends' help, so he told them all about Hiro.

"When Hiro broke down, his crew couldn't find the parts to fix him," Thomas explained. "Hiro was put in a siding and everyone forgot about him."

Gordon **gasped**! And James **jumped**! All the engines wanted to help Hiro.

The next few days on Sodor were busy. Gordon, James and Henry carried parts to Hiro, while Thomas puffed **up** and **down** his Branch Line.

After work, Thomas and Percy went to see Hiro.

The big engine was a colourful patchwork of parts. Hiro's firebox **fizzled** and **flared**. "I feel better already!" he smiled.

Suddenly there came a loud, **"Poop! Poop!"** Spencer had seen Hiro!

"What is that heap of scrap?" Spencer gasped. "Wait until I tell The Fat Controller."

Spencer **wheeshed** away, with Thomas chasing after. Thomas had to tell The Fat Controller about Hiro before Spencer did.

Suddenly, the old track gave way under Spencer. The big engine was **stuck**!

Thomas puffed on to Knapford, his **wheels wobbling**. When he arrived, he told The Fat Controller everything — all about Hiro and how Spencer had got stuck.

"Hiro was the Master of the Railway — I would never scrap him," The Fat Controller said kindly. "He must have been left there by accident. You must take Hiro to the Steamworks straight away, Thomas."

Soon Hiro was ready for action! His new boiler gleamed and his black paint shone. The Fat Controller asked Hiro to rescue Spencer.

"I'm sorry I was rude," said Spencer.

Hiro smiled. He felt stronger than ever! With a mighty **heave**, he pulled Spencer back on track.

"Well done, Hiro," peeped Thomas. "The Master of the Railway!"

More about Hiro

lamp

nameplate

boiler bands

cab

hand rail

buffer

coupling rod

coupling hook

Hiro's challenge to you

Look back through the pages of this book
and see if you can spot:

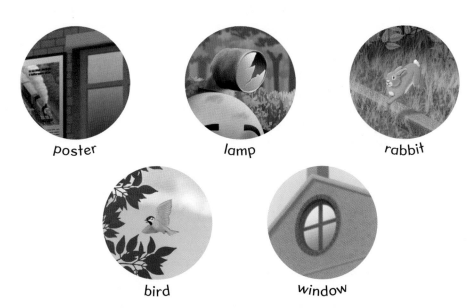

poster

lamp

rabbit

bird

window

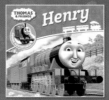

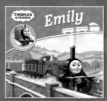